RIDING
THE TIGER

by
EVE BUNTING

with woodcuts by
DAVID FRAMPTON

CLARION BOOKS ◆ NEW YORK

Clarion Books
a Houghton Mifflin Company imprint
215 Park Avenue South, New York, NY 10003

Text copyright © 2001 by Eve Bunting
Illustrations copyright © 2001 by David Frampton

The illustrations were executed in woodcut.
The text was set in 14.5-point Romana.

Printed in the USA

Library of Congress Cataloging-in-Publication Data
Bunting, Eve, 1928–
Riding the tiger / by Eve Bunting ; illustrated by David Frampton.
p. cm.
Summary: Ten-year-old Danny is bored and lonely when he hops on the back of the
exciting and somewhat scary tiger that offers him a ride, but he soon discovers
that it's easier to get on the tiger than it is to get off.
ISBN 0-395-79731-4
[1.Tigers—Fiction. 2. Inner cities—Fiction.] I. Frampton, David, ill. II. Title.
PZ7.B91527 Rk 2001
[Fic]—dc21   00-043012

BVG 10 9 8 7 6 5 4 3 2

For all my grandchildren
—E.B.

To my kids
—D.F.

I was leaning against the wall of the house when the tiger came.

"Hi, Danny," he said.

It scared me that he knew my name, but I was pleased, too.

"A bit bored?" he asked. "A bit lonely?"

I nodded.

The tiger cocked his head. "That's the way it is when you're new in town. But we'll fix that. Why don't you hop on my back and we'll take a ride."

I stared at him.

He purred and rubbed his head against my shoulder. "Just a short ride. My back's wide and comfortable. And you've got nothing else to do, have you?"

"Well . . . I'll have to tell my mom where I'm going."

He grinned. "If you do, she won't let you."

I grinned back at him. "You're right about that. Okay."

He crouched so I could get on. My feet hung way off the ground, even though my legs are real long. Which is why my mom calls me Danny Long-Legs.

"Too bad you're not wearing my colors," the tiger said. "Next time."

"Sure," I said, not even knowing what colors he meant.

I held on to the thick, coarse fur at the tiger's neck. Each golden hair glistened. His black bands came together perfectly, like the stripes on a soccer jersey.

He smelled of something dark and exciting.

"Ready?" he asked.

"Ready."

"How old are you, Dan?"

"Ten," I said.

"Man, I'd have thought older."

Up there, high on his back, I did feel big, really big. I wanted to pound my chest and shout, "Look at me, everyone! I'm riding a tiger!"

An old man was reading his morning paper on the bench in front of Muto's grocery. When he saw us, he went inside, fast.

"Stay away from here!" he yelled.

The tiger turned to look at me. "That Muto is nothing but a wimp." His voice was the strangest mixture of every accent I'd ever heard.

A police car came cruising down the street. It slowed when the officers saw us.

12

"Hey, kid!" one of the officers called. "You're new, aren't you? You don't want to start off by riding that tiger. That's nothing but trouble."

"We're just taking a little walk, is all," the tiger said, quite politely. "To see if we like each other."

The officer looked closely at me. "Once you get up on the tiger's back, it's hard to get off. . . . But if you get off fast enough, it's still possible."

"He doesn't want to get off," the tiger said. "Right, Danny?"

I nodded. "Right."

But the officer and Mr. Muto had made me a bit edgy. Still, I didn't want to get off for a while. I didn't want the tiger to think I was a wimp, too.

The officer shrugged and the car rolled on.

The shops on Center Street were open for business. People moved off the sidewalk so the tiger and I could pass.

"This is neat," I whispered, and the tiger said, "Yeah! I always get respect. And whoever is with me gets respect, too."

Several kids said "Hi" to the tiger and looked enviously at me.

One girl touched his striped side and I felt him bristle.

"Can I go with you?" the girl asked.

"Not now," the tiger said. "Maybe later. Do you think the way I think?"

"Yes."

"Do you want what I want?"

The girl nodded.

"Because anyone who isn't for us is against us," the tiger said.

"I'm for you," the girl said, and the tiger lifted a paw, laid it on her shoulder.

"Come on over, then. You know where I'm at."

The tiger squinted back at me as we walked. "Questions that have to be asked," he said. "Pretty soon I'll be asking you."

16

We were passing a playground. A bunch of guys about my age were shooting baskets. They didn't even look up as we passed.

The tiger's lope turned to a swagger, which made it hard to stay on his back.

"Hey, pal," someone called. "You, on the tiger. Want to get off the beast and come play some ball?" The guy was older than the others. He could have been eighteen. His bare chest was brown and smooth as a nut.

"That's Ferdy," the tiger said. "He works at giving kids options."

The tiger said "options" as if it was the dumbest word that ever was. Were options the same as choices? I thought so. "He says there's lots of stuff that's more fun than riding the tiger." The tiger shook his head.

I leaned low across his neck. "To tell the truth I *do* like basketball. Maybe I will get off here. Thanks for the ride."

"But maybe I don't want you to get off," the tiger said. "Maybe I want to get to know you better."

My stomach gave a disgusting lurch.

"You didn't tell me I couldn't get off whenever I felt like it," I said.

"I don't tell everything," he said. "See those walls?"

I looked and saw that almost all the storefronts were covered with black tiger paw prints and words that I couldn't understand. The prints were on a McDonald's billboard, covering the slogan. They were written over a corner stop sign.

"That means we're in tiger territory," the tiger said. "Mine. Be honored you're with me."

But I wasn't honored anymore. I had to get off, here, where Ferdy was still watching and might help me. I brought my left leg up so I could slip down the tiger's side.

"Don't even think about it," the tiger said, and when he turned, I saw the yellow glitter of his eyes. I eased my leg back to where it had been before.

He was walking faster now and the ground seemed farther away. Had he grown bigger? Had I grown smaller? His paws made no sound; we flowed along in absolute silence.

Now there was a street jammed with traffic. Sometimes the tiger held up a paw so we could pass. One van driver didn't get out of his way fast enough.

"Move it!" the tiger snarled, and I heard the screech of something sharp digging into metal and saw where he'd raked the red paint off the van with his open claws.

Oh, man! I thought. That driver is going to tear us apart. But he just rolled up his window and turned his head away. His shoulders were hunched up around his ears.

"Now, that's respect," the tiger said.

But I knew right then it wasn't respect. It was something very different.

A Metro Line bus was moving slowly in front of us. What if I jumped for the step? But what if the driver wouldn't open the door? What if he turned his head away, like the guy in the van?

I didn't know where we were now, padding through
dark alleys, past rundown warehouses and loading docks.

A dog mooched away from us, its tail down.

A scattering of big crows cawed angrily and flopped up onto a
broken wall.

There was a bum, rooting through a garbage can. When he saw us, he began edging backward. But he edged too far, stepping behind him where there was only empty space.

I saw him fall. I heard the thud as he landed. Heard the quiet.

The tiger turned to grin at me and walked on.

"Wait!" I jerked at his neck fur. "The man's hurt. He needs help." I swung both legs down and hung, still clinging to the tiger's back.

"Stay where you are," the tiger said.

What if I didn't? What would he do to me? I heard his breathing, dark and deadly. And I heard a small whimper that could have been a cat but wasn't. It came from the man who'd fallen, too scared to make a noise, in too much pain to keep quiet.

I hung, halfway on and halfway off the tiger, and I knew I had an option. Which was the same as a choice. I glanced down. The ground was so far below me. Once you get up on the tiger's back, it's hard to get off. But if you get off fast . . .

I dropped. The concrete hit me like a pile driver. I fell over, stood again, dazed. Every bit of me hurt.

The tiger was in the shadow of one of the old buildings, a black giant of a creature. His tail moved gently.

I was trembling all over.

"You've had your chance. You'll never be one of us now," the tiger said. "Don't come whining and begging to me when you need help. You're all alone now, kid."

I licked my lips. "Maybe."

Then I was limping backward, waiting for the tiger to pounce, ready to run, jump, climb. But this was a tiger. How could I outpace him?

I risked turning my back on him, glancing down. The man lay at the bottom of crumbled steps, among empty bottles and candy wrappers.

When he saw me, he shielded himself with his arms.

"It's okay," I said. "I'm not with him."

And when I looked back, there were only three crows
strutting again in the alley and the dog nosing a cardboard box.

The tiger had gone.